Orangutan artist?

I flipped the page in my sketchbook.

"Hey, I *like* that one," Tyler said, pointing. "It's you, right?"

I looked down. It was a sketch of a person with red hair, eyes closed, head lying on arms. It was really crude—I mean, stick-figure crude. But there was something special about it.

"Wait a minute," I said, taking the pad from Tyler. "That's me. But I didn't do this. Who—"

"Zoey!" Tyler yelled.

I turned around. Zoey was smearing paint all over the wall next to my bed.

"Bad girl!" I yelled. "Give me that paintbrush!"

I reached forward and grabbed the brush from Zoey. She screeched and jumped into Tyler's arms.

"Look," Tyler said, pointing at the wall.

Zoey had drawn a stick figure on the wall—in exactly the same style as the figure with the red hair in my sketchbook.

Tyler and I looked at each other.

"You don't think . . ." I began.

"Yeah, I do," Tyler said. "Zoey did that painting."

Zoey & Me

Who Gave My Orangutan a Paintbrush?

Zoey & Me

Who Gave My Orangutan a Paintbrush?

MALLORY TARCHER

Troll

Text copyright © 1997 by Mallory Tarcher.
Cover illustration copyright © 1997 by Troll Communications L.L.C.

Published by Troll Communications L.L.C.

Cover illustration by Denise Brunkus.

Printed in the United States of America.

10 9 8 7 6 5 4 3 2

*For my orange friends at the Los Angeles Zoo
and for Birdie, for her time*

Chapter

1

Looking back, I guess it was all my fault. I'm the one who fell asleep.

It was a rainy Sunday night. I was sitting on my bed, trying to finish reading a book we were going to talk about in English class on Tuesday. The next thing I knew, it was morning, and my dad was calling me downstairs for breakfast.

The problem was that when I fell asleep, I left my watercolors out on the floor where anybody—and I do mean *anybody*—could get into them. And that's just what happened.

Of course, I didn't find out about it until Monday morning, when I had to get up at the ridiculously early hour of six A.M. Now that might not seem strange to some of you, but for me it was. Molly Miles (that's my name, don't wear it out) doesn't like mornings, or taking a shower, or having to make sure that all her clothes match. I don't even like breakfast all that much. Mornings are so hard for me that I don't even open my curtains after I get dressed (the light makes me cranky). That's why I didn't notice the mess Zoey had made.

Another weird thing about that day was that when I got downstairs at six-thirty, my Dad was already up—and he was baking.

"Dad, what are you doing? And where's Mom?" I asked. "She's supposed to drive Tyler and me to the Art Walk in"—I looked up at the clock—"twenty minutes."

"She's sleeping. One of the gorillas is sick, so she didn't get home from work until early this morning," Dad replied. "I'm taking you to the Art Walk. And I'm baking my world-famous peanut butter cookies for the bake sale table."

I smiled half-heartedly. I love my Dad, and he's a really good doctor, but baking is not one of his strong points. Still, it was nice of him to make the cookies. The Art Walk was an auction for charity. Each student in my school was supposed to bring in a painting, and each painting would be sold to the highest bidder. All the money was being donated to the Los Angeles Zoo. The auction committee had decided to have a bake sale table because people get hungry while they walk around looking at great works of art.

I opened the refrigerator door and tried to focus my sleepy eyes on the milk carton. There was a knock on the kitchen door. I looked up through my as-yet-uncombed hair and saw Tyler's face pressed against the back door window. His hair was all messed up, and he looked like he was having about as much fun being up this early as I was. I waved him inside.

It was strange to see Tyler walk into our house through a door, the way other people did. Lately he'd been using the trellis outside my bedroom window to come and go.

"Morning, Dr. Miles. Hi, Molly," he mumbled, shutting the door behind him. He was carrying a big, flat package wrapped in brown butcher paper under his arm.

Tyler Matthews is my best friend. He lives next door, and we've grown up together, played together, even taken vacations together. We've always been like brother and sister, except without the fighting part. Until lately, that is. Not that we've started arguing, but sometimes when I look at Tyler I notice how beautiful his eyes are, and I never ever think stuff like that about my real brother!

"Good morning, Tyler," Dad said. "Have a peanut butter cookie?" He held out the tray.

Tyler shook his head. "No, thanks," he replied quickly. He'd been one of Dad's victims in the past.

"So," I said, glancing at the package Tyler held. "Is that your painting?"

Tyler nodded.

"Mind if I take a look?"

"Go ahead." He unwrapped the package carefully, then held the painting up for me to see. It was a picture of a basketball player. He was sailing through the air as he slammed the ball through the net.

"It's nice," I remarked critically. "But nobody can jump that high."

"Michael Jordan can," Tyler stated matter-of-factly.

I frowned. "Who?"

11

Tyler looked at me like I'd grown two heads. "Michael Jordan. The basketball player?"

"Oh," I said. "Never heard of him."

"Never heard of him?" Tyler repeated again, continuing to look at me strangely.

This had started to happen a lot lately. One of us would say something that the other didn't get. That was strange. Tyler and I were always so tuned in to each other that we used to finish each other's sentences. I talked to Mom about it, but she didn't seem surprised. She told me it was because the differences between boys and girls got bigger as they got older. Personally, I just thought Tyler was getting weird. I knew I hadn't changed—at least I didn't think I had.

Tyler shook his head and sighed. "Never mind. Where's your painting?"

"Upstairs. I'll go get it."

"You'll eat breakfast first, young lady," Dad said sternly.

"Dad, I'm not eating cookies for breakfast," I replied self-righteously. I didn't bother telling him that if anyone other than he had baked those cookies, I would have already inhaled every one off the tray.

"Not cookies," Dad said as he pulled two clean plates out of the dishwasher. "Bacon-and-egg sandwiches." He popped open the microwave, pulled out two English muffin sandwiches, and slid them onto the plates. "Here, Tyler, have one."

"Wow," I remarked, taking a bite. "You made these?" I'd have to change my opinion of Dad's cooking if the peanut butter cookies were as good.

Dad laughed and held up the box the sandwiches had come in. "Even your old dad can be a great cook with these. Perfect every time."

Tyler and I wolfed our breakfast down in record time. "Come on," I said to him when we had finished. "Let's go get my painting. You can help me frame it."

"You haven't framed it yet?"

"I fell asleep last night while I was reading that boring book for English class," I told him honestly. "It'll just take a second."

"You'd better hurry," Dad said as he cleared the table. "We've got to leave in ten minutes." I nodded and led Tyler upstairs to my room.

The door was open a crack, which was odd. I didn't remember leaving it open. In fact, I remembered closing it tightly behind me. Anger started to build inside me as I wondered who had invaded my room. Whoever came in here must have mush for brains, I thought, looking at the huge KEEP OUT—THIS MEANS YOU sign that I'd hung in the middle of my door.

I pushed the door open wide and gasped as my eyes took in the incredible sight before me.

My room was a total disaster.

Chapter 2

Tyler and I stood in the doorway to my room, too stunned to go inside. A baby orangutan was sitting in the middle of the floor. My watercolor painting set was scattered all around her. She looked up at me, screeched, and smiled as she dabbed bright green paint on her knees.

"Zoey!" I yelled when I was finally able to talk again. "*What* are you doing?"

Zoey was the orangutan's name. And it wasn't as surprising as you might think for me to find her in my bedroom. After all, she did live with us.

You see, Zoey was more like my little sister than a pet. She'd been living with us now for almost a year, ever since her own mother at the zoo refused to take care of her. I thought that was the freakiest thing I'd ever heard of, but Mom says stuff like that happens sometimes with animals who grow up in cages. It's like they never learn how they're supposed to behave. Sometimes animals in captivity even forget things you'd think would come naturally to them, like raising a kid.

And my mom should know. She's a primatologist at

the Los Angeles Zoo. That means she knows a lot about all kinds of apes, including orangutans. So when Zoey's mom didn't want her, my mom decided we had to take Zoey in. Baby orangutans are a lot like human babies. They need constant care during their first years of life. If we hadn't cared for Zoey, well, she might not have made it.

The first few months Zoey lived with us were kind of fun. Every day, kids from school would stop by our house to see Zoey—especially after I made her my current events project at school one day. That's a whole long story I don't really want to get into right now, though.

Sometimes I hated having Zoey around. Until she came along I was the youngest in our family, and I was pretty spoiled. When Zoey arrived, Mom and Dad began treating me more like an adult. They gave me more responsibilities, and I had a hard time getting used to my new role in the family. After a while I got the hang of being a big sister, and I even started to enjoy bossing Zoey around (hey, you take what you can get). But she could still be a real pain sometimes. Like now.

"Look at what you've done," I scolded. My room looked like a little kid's finger-painting project. The white dresser was covered with splotches of red and blue. The dark green carpet now had a funky yellow and red and blue design, and one corner of my new patchwork quilt was dripping green paint.

"Ohhhh," I moaned, sitting down on the window seat. "This is going to take *forever* to clean up."

Zoey screeched happily. She didn't seem to care that she'd just ruined my life. In fact, she seemed pleased with herself.

"Hey, Zoey," Tyler cooed, kneeling down and holding out his arms. "Come here, girl."

As hard as it may be for you to believe, Zoey had a major crush on Tyler. She squealed with delight when she heard his voice. She bounded across the room in one leap and jumped into Tyler's waiting arms. He staggered backward and almost fell over.

Zoey snuggled into his arms as he struggled under her weight. "Wow," he said, smoothing the thin red hair that covered her head. "When did you learn how to jump like that?"

She screeched at him and smiled. Then she gave Tyler a wet, sloppy kiss that left him spluttering for mercy.

"Over the weekend," I murmured, still staring around at my room. "She was swinging from the chandelier all day yesterday."

In the jungle, orangutans almost never walk on the ground. The bottoms of their feet are actually curved. In the wild, they spend pretty much all their time swinging from tree to tree. Mom said that was one of the instincts captive orangutans didn't forget. We were going to have to get used to Zoey swinging all over the house from now on.

"Hey, what's all the racket about? It's only quarter to seven."

I turned and saw my older brother, Brad, standing in

the doorway. He looked as if he had just rolled out of bed. His blond hair was rumpled and had this funny spiky thing happening on the left side. The legs of his sweatpants were pushed up to his bony knees.

Brad was fifteen years old. Usually we got along pretty well, except when we fought about what to watch on TV. He always wanted to watch sports, especially baseball, or those action movies with Jean-Claude Van Damme.

"It's not my fault!" I cried. "Look at what Zoey did in here."

"Well, keep it down," Brad grumbled, rubbing his eyes. "Some of us are trying to sleep." He glared at me as he left the room. I glared right back. Like he didn't have to get up for school in fifteen minutes, anyway.

I had a sudden, horrifying thought. I ran over to my bed, reached underneath, and pulled out the sketchbook I'd done my painting in. The book was open to a blank page. My stomach started to hurt as I flipped the pages until I found my painting. It was perfect.

"My painting." I sighed with relief. "At least she didn't mess this up."

"Let me see," Tyler said, kneeling down. Zoey jumped out of his arms and up onto my bed. She lay down with her stuffed banana and started singing softly to herself.

"Here." I handed Tyler the sketchbook. He held my painting up before him and studied it.

It was a picture of two orangutans in the Indonesian jungle. I was pretty proud of it. I'd worked on it for the past week—not just painting the picture but doing research. I wanted to make all the details as accurate as possible. Whoever bought it would know exactly how orangutans lived in the wild.

I decided to do a painting of orangutans for a couple of reasons. One, the money collected from the Art Walk was going to the zoo. Two, Zoey is a great inspiration. I'd gone to the library and taken out some books on orangutans and the jungle, one of which, I saw, was lying on the floor with a big splotch of yellow paint on the cover. I made a mental note to clean it off before I returned the book.

"Cool," Tyler said, impressed. "I like the chimps best. And the trees look good, too."

"Chimps?" I frowned at him. "They're not chimps. They're orangutans."

"Oh, sorry," he said, peering more closely at the painting. "They don't look like Zoey."

"They do, too!" I snapped. "Well, maybe not exactly, but only because they're adults," I said, snatching the sketchbook back from Tyler. What did he know about orangutans, anyway? I flipped the page in the sketchbook.

"Hey, I *like* that one," Tyler exclaimed, pointing. "It's you, right?"

I looked down. Turning the page in the sketchbook had revealed another drawing—a watercolor smear of a person with red hair, eyes closed, head lying on arms. It was really crude—I mean, stick-figure crude. But there was something special about it.

"Wait a minute," I said. "That is me. But I didn't do this."

I frowned. Somebody had been coming into my room and using my paints. And there was only one person who would be sneaky enough to do that.

"Brad!" I yelled.

I heard a kind of groan come from his room. "What?" he yelled back.

"Leave my painting stuff alone! And stay out of my room!"

There was a minute of silence, then Brad appeared in my doorway again.

"I didn't touch your stupid painting stuff," he growled huffily.

"Right," I told him as I held up the painting. "I suppose Dad did this then?"

Brad rubbed his eyes and squinted at the sketchbook. "I don't know who did that," he replied. Then he smiled. "It's you studying, right? I can tell because your eyes are closed."

"Very funny," I said, glaring at him.

Brad glared right back. "Now, listen, Red. No more noise, or I won't let you watch any of your TV shows tonight. Got it?" Without waiting for an answer, he turned and disappeared down the hallway.

"You know, Molly," Tyler began. "I don't think Brad did that painting."

"Yeah, I think you're right," I agreed. "But then who—"

"Zoey!" Tyler yelled, cutting me off.

I turned around. Zoey had grabbed the paintbrush again, and now she was sitting on my dresser, smearing paint all over the wall next to my bed.

"Zoey!" I yelled. "Give me that! Bad girl."

I reached forward and grabbed the brush from her. She screeched and jumped into Tyler's arms again.

"Look," Tyler said, pointing at the wall.

Zoey had drawn a stick figure on the wall—in exactly the same style as the one with red hair in my sketchbook.

Tyler and I looked at each other disbelievingly. Zoey turned toward me and put her finger in her ear.

"You don't think . . ."

"Yeah, I do," Tyler said slowly. He reached down and ruffled Zoey's hair. "Looks like you're not the only artist in the family, Molly. Zoey did that painting in your sketchbook."

Chapter

3

For a minute, neither of us said a word.

"Hey, what's taking you two so long?" I looked up to find Dad standing in the doorway. "We've got to get going . . ." His voice trailed off as he surveyed the mess in my room.

"What happened in here?" he cried. I opened my mouth to explain, but just then Zoey jumped out of Tyler's arms, scooted past Dad, and ran down the hall into Brad's room.

"Never mind. I've got a pretty good idea who did this." Dad bent down and ran his hands along the paint-splotched carpet. "We've got to get this stuff up right away or it's going to stain."

"It's watercolor, Dad," I said. "It won't stain. Besides, we're already running late."

He held up a hand. "Better safe than sorry," he said, running his hands along the wall where Zoey had painted. "If your mother comes in here and sees this mess, we'll all be sorry we didn't clean it up right away."

"Dr. Miles," Tyler began excitedly, "you're not going to believe—"

I kicked him hard on his shin before he could finish his sentence.

"Ow!" Tyler yelped, staring at me. "What'd you do that for?"

I shook my head quickly, just as Dad turned back to us.

"What is it, Tyler?" he asked.

"Uhhh . . . nothing," Tyler mumbled. "I'll go get some cleaning supplies."

"Thanks. Show him where everything is Molly," Dad said. "If we all work together, we'll have this cleaned up in no time."

"But, Dad, I still have to frame my painting," I reminded him.

"I'll take care of it," Dad replied. "Now, you two get going or we're going to be really late."

I led Tyler down to the laundry room to get the cleaning supplies.

"Why'd you kick me?" Tyler asked as he massaged his shin.

"Because I didn't want you to tell my dad about Zoey's painting," I explained. "I want to show my mom first."

Tyler stared at me the same way he had when I said I'd never heard of Michael Jordan—like I was from Mars. It was kind of a hard thing to understand, I guess, but I wanted to prove to Mom that I was proud of Zoey. There were times before, I know, when it must have seemed to Mom that I didn't want Zoey around at all. I knew that stressed her out, and I wanted to show her I'd changed.

If fact, after Zoey's first few months with us, I spent most of my time complaining about her. Not that she wasn't a total pain at times. She ate my homework, and once I found my entire collection of horse statues balanced on the ceiling fan—and they were all covered in orangutan spit! Mom got tired of my whining and finally stopped listening to it. For the last month or two I'd tried to find ways to praise Zoey whenever Mom was around. Now I had something really big to tell her.

"All right," Tyler said finally. "No big deal."

"Thanks." I smiled. It might not have been a big deal to him, but it was to me.

It didn't take as long as I thought to clean up my room. We were only about twenty minutes behind schedule when Dad finally pulled the minivan out of the driveway.

By the time we drove into the school parking lot, preparations for the Art Walk were in full swing. The only place in the school big enough to have the show was the gym, which needed a lot of work to turn it into a gallery to display all the students' paintings. We walked in and saw teachers and students hard at work putting up metal framing to hang everybody's paintings from. The place looked kind of like the framework of a house before the walls are put up. In this case, the walls were going to be all the paintings.

A big banner that said ART WALK—FOR THE BENEFIT OF THE LOS ANGELES ZOO was hanging across the center of the gym. I was staring up at the banner, which had pictures of lions, elephants, and chimpanzees (but no orangutans) on it, when I heard somebody call my name.

"Molly, Tyler—over here!"

I turned and saw Mrs. Hurwitz, our homeroom teacher, waving at us.

"Sorry we're late," I blurted as we walked up to her. "Zoey—"

"Ah." Mrs. Hurwitz smiled. "No explanations necessary." And they weren't. Mrs. Hurwitz had been involved in that story about Zoey as my current events project that I really don't want to talk about right now. "I'm just glad you're here," she said as she handed each of us a name tag. "There are a million things to do before we open up." Tyler and I had volunteered to help set up for the Art Walk, and that's why we were at school so early.

My dad strode up to us a moment later. "Hello, Dr. Miles." Mrs. Hurwitz smiled. "How are you this morning?"

"Just fine, Mrs. Hurwitz," Dad replied, smiling back at her. He reached into the big shopping bag he was carrying and pulled out our paintings. "I suppose you want these."

"Yes, I do," she said. "I'm very much looking forward to seeing them."

"And that's only part of what I have for you," Dad continued mischievously. He reached into the bag and pulled out a tray covered with aluminum foil. "May I present—"

"Your famous peanut butter cookies," Mrs. Hurwitz said, finishing his sentence. "What a nice treat."

"You remembered!" Dad smiled, obviously pleased that my teacher hadn't forgotten his past baking efforts.

Mrs. Hurwitz smiled back—at least, I think it was a smile. "We *all* remember your peanut butter cookies, Dr. Miles." She took the tray from him and handed it to one of the class mothers.

"Well, good luck, everyone," Dad said. "Molly, I'll see you at dinner." I waved good-bye to him, then turned back to my teacher.

"What do you need us to do, Mrs. Hurwitz?" Tyler asked.

She thought for a minute before speaking. "Tyler, why don't you hunt down Mrs. Walsh and help her put up paintings on the scaffolding? And, Molly, we could use you at the ticket-takers' booth, around the front of the gym."

"Okay," I agreed. "See you later, Ty."

We'd come in through the back entrance to drop off our paintings, so I had to walk all the way around to the front, doing my best to keep out of everybody's way. Lots of kids and their parents had come to set up, and the gym looked great. I stopped a few times to admire the paintings that had already been hung.

When I finally made it to the front of the gym, a nasty little surprise was waiting for me. There, putting pink ribbons around the edge of the ticket booth, was Margie Lussman.

Now, let me say right away that I don't hate anybody. But some people rub me the wrong way, and Margie was definitely one of those people. In addition to

25

coming from the richest family in town (and always making sure everybody knew it), Margie never had anything nice to say about anybody.

She was extra mean to me because Tyler and I were friends. Margie had a huge crush on Tyler, and it killed her to see me hanging around with him. I guess she thought we were more than best friends. I should have told her we weren't, but I kind of liked seeing her get mad when we were together.

I took a deep breath. "Hi, Margie. How's it going?" I smiled through clenched teeth.

She turned around and flashed the biggest smile I had ever seen. I was amazed. Margie was in a good mood.

She sure was dressed for something special, in a fancy blue dress with a wide collar. I looked down at my jeans and faded sweatshirt and thought about going home to change.

"So, did you hear?" Margie gushed. "Isn't it just the most exciting thing?"

I stared at Margie, not quite sure what she was talking about. I finally managed to mumble a quick "Uhhh" before she continued.

"You mean, you don't know?" Margie's eyes were bright with excitement. "Georges Edward is coming to our the Art Walk!" She pronounced the name "George S. Edward" and practically drooled as she finished.

I thought a minute. Georges Edward, Georges Edward.

"Oh, right," I said. I remembered him now. Georges

Edward was one of those guys who always appeared on the entertainment segments of the news. He hung out with movie stars and supermodels, and he always wore black. "I know him," I told Margie. "He's the guy with the beret."

"The guy with the beret!" Margie sniffed. "He's not just the guy with the beret. He's the best, the most famous, and the cu-*u*-test"—she dragged out the *u* so long I thought I would puke—"artist there is. And he'll be here at one o'clock this afternoon."

"As long as he has the admission price," I reminded her, taking a seat behind the booth. I looked up at the big clock on the wall. Almost eight. We were supposed to open at nine. All around the gym, people were hard at work putting up the framing, hanging paintings, and setting up tables. And here I was, stuck listening to Margie drone on and on about how wonderful Georges Edward was. I was bored stiff.

Till the doors opened. Then Margie and I were the busiest people in the place.

I don't know if the school had expected so many people, but I hadn't. I must have sold five hundred tickets. And the whole time, Margie kept talking about how exciting it was going to be when Georges Edward showed up that afternoon. It hardly seemed possible the whole morning had passed when Mrs. Hurwitz came by and told us it was time to break for lunch. She also handed us a tray full of cookies.

"Leftovers from the bake sale," she explained. "I figured you two deserved them."

I looked at the tray. Most of it was filled with the peanut butter cookies Dad had made.

"Wow." Margie eyed the tray hungrily. "Peanut butter cookies." She looked up at me. "I shouldn't," she said quietly.

Did I tell you that Margie was fat? It was one of the few things I actually liked about her.

"Oh, go on," I purred. "They won't kill you."

"They're a little dry," Mrs. Hurwitz said. Then she looked at me. "Which is not to say they're not delicious," she quickly added, remembering who had baked them.

I smiled and grabbed half a muffin off the tray.

"See you later, girls." Mrs. Hurwitz waved as she walked back into the gym.

Margie promptly dug into the peanut butter cookies.

"Want one?" she asked.

"No, I'm fine. Help yourself."

"Molly." I looked up, startled. Brad was standing in front of the ticket booth.

"You've got to pay to get in, Brad," Margie mumbled through a mouthful of cookie.

"Buzz off, Lussman," Brad snarled. "I'm not here for the Art Walk. I'm here to talk to my sister."

Then I saw who he had with him. An orange face peeked over Brad's shoulder. Zoey was tucked in her little blue baby carrier.

"Oh, no," I groaned. If Brad was here with Zoey, that could only mean one thing.

"You have to take her," Brad pleaded. "Mom had to go back to the zoo again, so she left Zoey with me. But I have practice, and I can't take her."

"Wait a minute," I said suspiciously. "You have baseball practice at lunch?"

"I only had a half day of school today," Brad bragged. I had forgotten that the high school kids got off early that day because they had to take some special tests. I hoped Brad flunked.

"It's extra batting practice. We have our regular practice this afternoon. Come on," he begged. "It's just for an hour. I'll be back at"—he looked at the clock—"one-fifteen."

"Well . . ." I considered. Things had slowed down. And if Brad would be back in an hour . . .

Well, what could happen in an hour?

"You're not bringing that monkey in here," Margie declared huffily.

I was about to tell her off when a thought occurred to me.

"Margie," I said. "I have a great idea."

She looked at me suspiciously. "What?"

I cleared my throat. "This whole Art Walk is for the benefit of the zoo, right?"

Margie nodded slowly, not wanting to agree with me.

"Well," I continued. "Wouldn't it be great if next week's issue of the school paper had a picture of some of the volunteers with a symbol of what the Art Walk is trying to benefit?"

"You mean Zoey?" Margie asked.

I nodded.

She crossed her arms and stared at Zoey, who was trying to braid Brad's hair with her toes.

"Come on, Margie," I pleaded. Then I had another thought. "Mr. Edward might want his picture taken with Zoey, too. It would be great publicity for him."

Margie's eyes lit up. "Really? You think so?"

"I don't know," Brad said, stepping in. "But I do know Tony White—he's the editor of your school paper. If I talk to him, he'll get a photographer over here for sure."

I smiled at Brad. I knew he was desperate to get to practice, so he'd go along with anything I said.

"Wow." Margie's eyes gleamed. "Maybe I can have my picture taken with Zoey and Mr. Edward. Cool."

"I'll get Tony to send a photographer," Brad assured her. He handed me Zoey and the baby carrier. "Bye, Red. And thanks."

"Bye," I replied through gritted teeth. If I've told Brad once I've told him a million times that I *hate* being called Red!

The next half hour dragged. I spent most of the time playing with Zoey, and Margie spent most of it fixing her makeup (which, by the way, I wasn't allowed to wear to school for another two years) and getting ready for the photographer.

But the photographer wasn't the next person to show up. Mrs. Hurwitz was. Along with a very stylish-looking man and woman, both dressed all in black.

Mrs. Hurwitz stood in front of the booth. "Here she is, Mr. Edward—"

Margie stepped forward, a big smile on her face. "Oh, Mr. Edward, I'm honored to meet you."

"Molly Miles," Mrs. Hurwitz finished. "She's the one who did the painting."

Margie's face fell. My mouth dropped to the floor.

"Young girl," Mr. Edward boomed, stepping forward. He had a French accent, so he pronounced *girl* like *garl*. "You are a genius."

"I am?" He was wearing his usual black beret, and he wasn't as tall as I had expected, probably only about five feet eight or so. He was thin, and his blond stringy hair hung limply around his face. The woman standing behind him was even thinner. She looked down at a little notepad.

"Mr. Edward," she squeaked, studying her watch. It sounded like her throat was all pinched up. That's how her face looked, too. "We have only five more minutes here. Then we have to leave for the conference."

Mr. Edward nodded. "Thank you, Helene." He turned toward me again and smiled. He had a mouth full of big white teeth that were so obviously fake I wanted to laugh. He also reeked of aftershave.

Plus, he wasn't really cute at all.

Margie thought otherwise, though.

"Oh, Mr. Edward," she gushed, stepping in front of me. "I think your artwork is the greatest."

"But of course," he agreed. "I am always glad to meet the young people." Brushing past Margie, he turned his attention back to me.

"Now, as I was saying—"

At that second Zoey, who had been sitting in my lap, jumped up and screeched.

"An ape!" Mr. Edward gasped, startled. He took a step backward and stumbled. The beret fell off his head and slid to the floor.

In one fluid motion Zoey darted off my lap, grabbed the beret, and ran off into the middle of the gym.

"Someone stop that monkey!" Mr. Edward shouted as he ran after her.

I groaned and hid my face in my hands. I was wrong. With Zoey around, a lot could happen in an hour.

Chapter 4

I didn't want to look. Zoey was ruining my day yet again. But the tone of Mrs. Hurwitz's voice snapped me to attention.

"Oh, dear," she was muttering, shaking her head. "Oh, dear."

You have to understand, Mrs. Hurwitz is very calm. That from her is practically panic.

I looked up. Right after grabbing Mr. Edward's beret, Zoey must have jumped onto the nearest section of metal framework. She had quickly climbed up to the top. Now she was gripping the metal frame with her toes, rocking back and forth and screeching loudly.

That frame had to be at least twelve feet tall. I didn't know how sturdy it was, and I didn't know how good a climber Zoey was. She'd only started swinging from the chandelier this past weekend, so I was really afraid she might fall and get hurt.

"Zoey!" I yelled. "Come down from there!"

She looked at me, screeched, and put the beret in her mouth.

"Leave that alone, you monkey!" Mr. Edward screamed. He was shaking his fist at Zoey.

"She's not a monkey," said a familiar-sounding voice. I turned and saw Tyler standing behind me. "She's an orangutan."

"Well, whatever kind of creature she is, she is ruining a very expensive beret," the woman with Mr. Edward replied.

This was not good. It seemed like everyone in the entire gym was gathering around us and staring up at Zoey. Her legs started to tremble, and I could tell she was beginning to get a little scared.

"Come on, Zoey," I said, more quietly this time. "Come down."

Zoey looked at me and screeched again. It seemed as if she was listening to me now.

"Come here," I repeated, holding my arms out.

Zoey jumped. Right off the frame. Right into the air.

I held my breath and prayed she wouldn't fall to the ground. She didn't. Somehow Zoey managed to land on another part of the framework. It swayed under the impact of her weight. The scaffolding she'd jumped off fell crashing to the ground, along with the dozen or so paintings that were hanging from it.

"Dear me," Mrs. Hurwitz moaned under her breath.

By now, everyone was watching Zoey. She was walking across the framework, which was swaying back and forth. I had to do something quickly before she got hurt. And before she really did some damage.

I grabbed Tyler's arm. "Come on," I said. "We have to get her down."

"I'm with you. But how?"

I looked around, trying to think of something clever to do. All I came up with was a lot of nothing.

"Well, we'll just have to climb up and carry her down," I decided. And before anyone could talk me out of it, I took a deep breath and pulled myself up on the scaffolding.

"Be careful, Molly," I heard Mrs. Hurwitz say.

The framework was light, but it felt pretty sturdy. My big worry was whether or not my weight plus Zoey's was going to tip it over. Tyler shot me a nervous look.

"Is it going to hold?" he asked.

"I think so," I said shakily. "As long as you come over here and balance it."

"Come on," Tyler said, turning and pointing to some of the people who'd gathered behind us. I recognized Billy Delaney and Chuck Donovan and Andrea Gordon from our class. There were a whole bunch of other people, too. They all walked forward and grabbed either side of the scaffolding.

"Go on, Molly!" Andrea shouted. "Go get her!"

I smiled down at her, took a deep breath, and began to climb.

Zoey was about five feet above me. The framework was still swaying, but I could feel people steadying it— so many of them, I realized, that even if I fell, I was sure to land on one of them instead of the floor.

I risked a look up at Zoey. She was still chewing on the beret, glancing around nervously.

"Zoey!" I shouted. "Come down—right now!"

She looked at me, screeched, and jumped straight up in the air.

"Oh, no," I muttered, bracing myself for the worst. Zoey was going to land on the floor and really hurt herself. Zoey was going to knock over another bunch of paintings, and this time, someone was going to get hurt. Zoey was . . .

She landed back on the framework, surefooted as a cat.

The whole thing shook, and for a second I thought I was going to lose my grip. Then the shaking stopped, and I steadied myself.

"Zoey!" I yelled. "Bad girl! Bad!"

She looked at me kind of sadly. I guess my tone of voice had finally gotten through to her. She hopped across the frame, bent over, put her arms around my neck, and hugged me.

The beret dropped to the floor. Out of the corner of my eye, I saw Margie "Kiss-Up" Lussman hurry over to retrieve it. She fluffed it up before handing it to Mr. Edward.

"That's a good girl," I cooed to Zoey as I started to climb down.

It took me about twice as long to get down, not surprising considering I had a thirty-pound orangutan hanging off my back. By the time I got to the ground, I was sweating. I was also grateful that Zoey hadn't been hurt.

"Are you all right?" Mrs. Hurwitz asked as relief flooded her face.

I nodded. "I'm fine. But look at this mess. Everything is ruined!"

I pointed at the scaffolding Zoey had knocked over. A small group of students began picking up the paintings that had been scattered across the floor.

Zoey, as if sensing she'd done something wrong, cuddled closer to me.

"The paintings are fine, Molly," Mrs. Hurwitz assured me. "And as long as Zoey is okay . . ."

"She's okay." I smiled, staring down at the little imp in my arms, who was looking about as cute right now as she ever had. I decided not to kill her when I got home that night.

Zoey looked up at Mrs. Hurwitz, screeched, and smiled. Mrs. Hurwitz took her in her arms.

"Young lady." I turned to see Mr. Edward standing in front of me. "Now I am late for my two o'clock."

I stared at him. Like I cared.

"Molly," Mrs. Hurwitz began, stepping forward before I could say what was on my mind. I guess she must have seen the look on my face. "I know you'll want to thank Mr. Edward for the *very* generous contribution he's made to the zoo by buying your painting for five hundred dollars."

Tyler's eyes bugged out. I'm sure mine did, too.

"Five hundred dollars!" I gasped. "Ummm . . ."

I looked at Mr. Edward, unsure of what to say. I mean, I liked my painting and all, but five hundred dollars? I tried to think about what Mom might say in a situation like this.

"Thank you so much, Mr. Edward," I said. "For myself, and especially for the zoo." I smiled. "I'm sure even Zoey thanks you."

He raised an eyebrow. "I care little for the opinion of this chimpanzee. But I know great art when I see it, and I like to see that kind of talent recognized."

Zoey's an orangutan, I thought to myself. I gritted my teeth and said nothing. All right, money bought my silence.

"I'm curious." Mr. Edward leaned closer. His aftershave was so strong, I was beginning to get woozy. "What made you decide to do a self-portrait?"

"A self-portrait?"

"Most of the other art I see here is of famous people or animals. *Pfui!*" He almost spit when he said the word. "It takes a true artist to search for the human being inside herself."

I felt Tyler's hand on my shoulder, and I suddenly had a sinking feeling in the pit of my stomach.

"Mr. Edward, could I see the picture you bought?" I asked.

Mrs. Hurwitz frowned and stepped forward. "Is there a problem, Molly?"

"Oh, no," I said quickly. "I just want to take one last look at it. You know, before Mr. Edward leaves with it."

"Of course." Mr. Edward's fake teeth filled his face. "I know it is sometimes difficult to part with one's artwork. It's like letting go of a part of one's self." He snapped his fingers, and from out of nowhere Helene produced the painting.

I had to fight pretty hard to keep my emotions from showing.

The painting he'd paid five hundred dollars for was Zoey's, not mine.

Chapter 5

"**Y**ou paid five hundred dollars for this . . . uh, p-painting?" I stammered.

"Yes," Mr. Edward said proudly. He held up the painting with one hand. With his other, he pointed at the red circles around my head that—I guess—were supposed to represent my hair. "This area immediately captured my attention because of these bold, sweeping lines."

"The texture." Helene sighed. "So organic."

She, too, was studying the painting like it was the Mona Lisa or something. How upset would they be if they knew an orangutan had painted it?

"Oh, yes." That was Tyler. He stepped forward, a little smile on his face. "Real organic."

I glared at him.

Mr. Edward spoke again. "This would go wonderfully with the Kennedy sculptures, don't you think, Helene? In the main entrance hall? A joint display?"

"Oh, yes, Mr. Edward," Helene agreed, nodding. "I'll get James on it right away." She hurriedly scribbled something in her personal organizer, then snapped it shut.

"Do that," Mr. Edward said. "I'd like to have it in place for the opening."

"The opening of your new gallery, right?" Margie pushed her way between Tyler and me. "I read about it in the paper last week. It sure sounds like it's going to be an exciting party."

"Yes, I'm very much looking forward to it," he replied. "It's time for the world to see the personal treasures of Georges Edward."

"I'd love to see them," Margie said hopefully.

"By invitation only," Helene responded firmly. Margie stared at her. If looks could kill, Helene would have been six feet under.

Just then there was a loud beeping sound. Helene reached into her purse, pulled out a cellular phone, and began speaking into it.

"It's a very inspiring work, Molly," Mr. Edward commented, putting the painting down. He started to wrap it back up.

Zoey, who'd been sitting quietly in Mrs. Hurwitz's arms, suddenly leaned forward and screeched.

Mrs. Hurwitz laughed. "I don't think she wants you to sell it, Molly."

If only you knew, I thought. I realized what must have happened. Dad must have thought Zoey's painting was mine, so that was the picture he framed. Then Mrs. Hurwitz put it on display with the others.

I could straighten this out in a minute.

"Are you all right, Molly?" Mrs. Hurwitz asked. "You look a little pale."

"No, I'm fine," I said. "But there's been a little mix-up. You see—"

"Mr. Edward, the conference chairwoman is on the line," Helene interrupted. "They'll hold the conference for you. But we have to go now."

Mr. Edward nodded. "I have to go. But thank you so much for your painting, Molly—exquisite!"

With that, he turned on his heel and left, trailing a cloud of aftershave behind him.

"Ohhh," Margie sighed, gawking after him. "He's *so* handsome."

"He's a creep," I muttered.

"I'm afraid he is a rather disagreeable man," Mrs. Hurwitz said. "Still, he did spend quite a bit of money on your painting, Molly. That guarantees the Art Walk is going to be a major success! Now we can do one of these every year." She was happier than I'd ever seen her. For a minute I thought she was going to hug me.

But instead she just smiled, handed Zoey to Tyler, and walked off.

I stared after her. Now what was I going to do?

"Molly," Tyler whispered.

I turned to look at him. "What?"

He shook his head quickly back and forth, almost as if he was afraid someone would notice. "You're not thinking of telling Mr. Edward that Zoey painted the picture he bought, are you?"

"I sure am."

"Are you crazy?" Tyler asked. He leaned in closer. "Listen. The fact is, if Mr. Edward finds out that an orangutan painted the picture he just spent *five hundred dollars* on"—Tyler drew out each word to emphasize it—"he'll want his money back faster than you can say *orangutan*. And that would be really bad publicity for the Art Walk. It'd look like we tried to cheat him or something." He smiled. "You know, make a monkey out of him."

"Very funny, Tyler," I hissed. "So what am I supposed to do when my parents congratulate me for selling my painting? Lie? I'm not going to do that."

Zoey, who was sitting happily in Tyler's arms, began screeching quietly to herself as she tried to undo his shirt buttons with her toes.

"And how can I not tell my mom that Zoey painted a picture?" I asked. "Do you know how excited she's going to be about that?"

He stared at me and shook his head slowly.

"I don't know," Tyler said. "But I could see it ruining the whole Art Walk if Mr. Edward wants his money back. They might never do another one."

He had a point. My head was starting to hurt from all the arguing.

"I'll think about it," I said finally.

"Hey, what's up, guys?"

I turned and saw Brad walking toward the booth.

"Not your photographer friend," Margie snarled. "What about getting my picture taken with Mr. Edward?"

Brad shrugged his shoulders. "I told Tony the guy was coming. That's the best I could do."

"Well, it wasn't good enough," Margie shot back. Tyler and I exchanged glances. Like she would have ever gotten a picture with Mr. Edward, anyway.

"How was Zoey?" Brad asked me.

I sighed and flopped down in my chair. "You don't want to know," I told him.

"Ah, she couldn't have been that bad," he said. He grabbed her from Tyler, and she immediately started grooming his hair. "She seems pretty calm to me."

"Sure, now she's well behaved," I grumped.

"Hey, you guys had better clean this place up," Brad called over his shoulder as he left with Zoey. "There's a bunch of people getting ready to come in."

I turned and saw that he was right. Through the gym doors, I could see a whole new group of people— the after-lunch crowd—heading for the gym. We were going to get busy again.

Suddenly I was starving. I needed something to get my energy going.

There was one of Dad's peanut butter cookies left on the tray that Mrs. Hurwitz had brought us.

What the heck, I thought. I picked it up and took a big bite.

"*Blecch,*" I spluttered, practically spitting it out. It tasted like sandpaper.

Which fit my mood perfectly.

Chapter 6

Tyler and I ended up staying at school till almost five o'clock, helping to clean up after the Art Walk. It had been very successful. I overheard Mrs. Hurwitz tell another teacher that they'd made a lot of money for the zoo.

Brad's newspaper friend finally sent the photographer by. He took some pictures of Margie and me at the ticket booth, and that made the rest of the time we spent together that afternoon almost pleasant. Everything would have been great if Margie hadn't bored me to sleep with the millions of pictures she took on her family's latest vacation. Luckily there weren't many pictures of Margie.

Still, by the time Tyler's parents dropped me off at home, I was exhausted. I just wanted to veg out in front of the TV and do a little more thinking about the horrible spot I was in. Nobody else was due home till around six: Brad had baseball practice, Dad was picking him up after work, and Mom was still stuck at the zoo, taking care of the sick gorilla. I didn't really know who Zoey was with, but I didn't care. I was just glad she wasn't with me. I'd had enough of her earlier in the day.

That left me the next hour or so at home alone with my conscience. I definitely needed to put on the TV and turn up the sound to drown out my guilty feelings.

Despite what Tyler thought, I knew the right thing was to tell Mr. Edward that Zoey had really done the painting. Even if a lot of bad things happened because of that, Mom always said honesty was the best policy—wasn't it?

But what if my honesty ended up costing the zoo five hundred dollars? What if there was never another Art Walk? How could that be the best policy?

I knew I should at least tell Mom about Zoey doing the painting. That was a radical scientific development that she'd definitely need to know about. On the other hand, if it was so radical, she could hardly keep it a secret, could she? No. Then Mr. Edward would find out, and the zoo would lose five hundred dollars. Back to square one.

Was that the right thing to do?

I decided to talk to Brad when he got home. He usually had good advice to give me. That is, when he wasn't being a fifteen-year-old know-it-all.

My head started to hurt. And I was hungry, so I went into the kitchen to grab some pretzels to tide me over until dinner.

Just then, the doorbell rang.

I wondered who it could be. Tyler would go to the back door or climb up the trellis, but he'd never ring the doorbell. And let's face it, I didn't have a ton of other friends at school. Maybe it was Margie Lussmann coming to beg for more peanut butter cookies. More likely it was somebody for Brad—probably a girl. Honestly, I had no idea why so many girls thought Brad was cute. They obviously hadn't taken the time to get to know him.

When I opened the door, I got the surprise of my life. It wasn't one of Brad's lovesick groupies. It was Mr. Georges Edward, his assistant, Helene, and Mrs. Hurwitz.

My heart sank to my toes. It's bad enough when a teacher sends a note home to your parents. I knew I was in huge trouble if Mrs. Hurwitz had come to see Mom and Dad in person.

"Hello, Molly," Mr. Edward said, walking past me. "What a charming home you have."

There could be only one reason they'd shown up here. Somehow they'd found out that Zoey had really done the painting. Now Mr. Edward was going to give it back, and he was going to take back the money he'd paid for it. I was going to be exposed as a liar in front of the whole school, and my life would be ruined.

Funny, though. They didn't look mad.

"Hello, Molly." Mrs. Hurwitz was smiling. "Are your parents home? Mr. Edward would like to speak with them."

"Mr. Edward has had a brilliant idea," Helene announced. She had changed into a man's gray business suit, which looked like it was about two sizes too big. She was wearing bright red lipstick and what

47

smelled like a gallon of perfume. My eyes started to water from the overpowering scent.

"Yes. A brilliant idea," Mr. Edward agreed. He had on the same gray suit as Helene, although he wasn't wearing lipstick. He was, however, wearing the same perfume. Either that, or she was just wearing so much of it that I couldn't smell anything else.

He bent to sit down on our living room chair, then ran a finger along the cushion.

"Is this an imitation?" he asked me. "Or the real thing? Van Diesenberg? Nineteen thirties, yes?"

"Uhhh . . ." I shook my head. I had no idea what he was talking about.

"Never mind." Mr. Edward waved his hand in the air and sat down. "I want you," he announced, "to paint my portrait for my gallery opening next Monday night—a week from today."

My mouth dropped open. "M-Me?" I stammered.

Mr. Edward nodded. So did Helene and Mrs. Hurwitz, who was still smiling.

"I need a fresh, young look," he explained.

"And you are young," Helene said. "Mr. Edward has always believed in sponsoring young artists."

"Sponsoring?" My mind was reeling. He wanted another painting?

"Sponsoring. One thousand dollars," he said. "Your style is unique. Primitive. It's the look I want for the gallery. And for my winter line of clothes."

"Especially the winter line," Helene added.

"A thousand dollars." I couldn't believe what I was

hearing. This was too much. I had to tell him the truth about the painting, right here and now.

"Mr. Edward," I began, taking a deep breath, "I can't take your money. You see—"

"A true artist! I admire that," he declared, standing up and straightening his beret. "We'll donate it to a worthy cause, then. The school?" he asked Helene.

Mrs. Hurwitz beamed.

Helene shook her head. "The zoo. The publicity will be even better."

Mrs. Hurwitz stopped smiling, but there wasn't much she could say without sounding mean.

"I have another brilliant idea," Mr. Edward boomed. "We will turn the whole opening into a benefit for the zoo! Primitive Art—for the primitives!"

"Mr. Edward," I said, trying again.

"This may be just the press angle we need." Helene thought for about five seconds. "It *is* another brilliant idea!" She reached into her briefcase and pulled out a gray envelope.

I was looking back and forth between them so fast my eyeballs were getting sore.

She handed the envelope to me. "Here are a dozen photos of Mr. Edward in various poses."

"Mr. Edward," I tried once more. "I—"

"We want a head and shoulders shot," Helene continued. "No beret."

"Helene," Mr. Edward said, standing suddenly. "I've changed my mind."

"Mr. Edward!" she cried, a shocked expression on

her face. "Are you sure about this?"

He nodded, his face very serious. "Quite sure."

She nodded right back, her expression equally serious. Then Helene turned to me. "Do it with the beret."

"It makes me look heroic," Mr. Edward stated. Then he frowned. "But I don't want to be too heroic. You know, I need less Christian Slater, more . . ." He stopped, searching for a word.

"Stallone?" Helene suggested.

Mr. Edward shook his head. "No."

"Bruce Willis?"

"No," he growled, frowning. "A thousand no's."

"Clark Gable?" Mrs. Hurwitz asked.

Mr. Edward sniffed. "Not quite."

I wasn't exactly sure who they were talking about. Some old movie star, I guessed.

Helene thought a minute. "Jim Carrey?"

"Yes!" he exclaimed, smiling. "That's it exactly."

Stop! I shouted, holding up my hands.

To my surprise, everyone did.

"There's something I have to tell you," I said in a much softer voice. "You see—"

Just then the front door burst open, and my parents and Brad walked in.

"Oh, Molly," Mom said. She was beaming. "I heard the great news about your painting . . ."

Her voice trailed off as she saw Mrs. Hurwitz, Mr. Edward, and Helene standing in the middle of our living room.

"Hello," she greeted them. "You're Georges Edward."

Mr. Edward bowed. "I am."

My dad joined the group and extended his hand.

"Welcome to our home, Mr. Edward. I'm Charles Miles. This is my wife, Sara, and my son, Brad. And I know you've already met Molly. Hi, Mrs. Hurwitz."

My dad gave me his "Is there something you want to tell us before anyone else does?" look. In turn, I gave him my best innocent face. He frowned. That face always made him nervous.

Mr. Edward took Dad's outstretched hand and shook it. He smiled at Mom.

"Your daughter is quite talented, Mrs. Miles. Quite talented."

Brad stepped forward just then. Zoey, who was strapped into the backpack, peered nosily over his shoulder.

Mr. Edward caught sight of her and took a step back. "The monkey!" he cried. "Keep it away from me!"

"She's an orangutan. But don't worry. Zoey's harmless," Brad assured Mr. Edward. As if to prove his point, Zoey leaned over and gave Brad a sloppy, wet kiss. He laughed. Mr. Edward didn't.

"Harmless! That creature ruined my beret!" Mr. Edward glared at Zoey, who glared right back at him.

"It looks all right to me," Dad commented as he examined the beret on Mr. Edward's head.

Mr. Edward turned to him and shook his head. "This is a different one."

Mom smiled politely. "I'm sorry your beret was

ruined, Mr. Edward," she began. "Zoey's just going through a phase. By the way, what brings you all here?"

"Mr. Edward has had a brilliant idea," Helene said.

"Yes, it is brilliant."

And then they explained how they wanted me to do Mr. Edward's portrait for the gallery opening the following Monday, and how they would donate a thousand dollars to the zoo if I agreed. As they talked, I could tell that my parents were really proud of me and that Brad was more than a little jealous. Both things I would normally be very pleased about. But right now I was trying to wrap my mind around this huge problem. If I agreed to paint the picture, they'd figure out I was a fraud as soon as they saw it. If I said no, they'd know sooner.

"It sounds terrific to me," Dad was saying. Then he caught sight of the expression on my face. "But of course, it's up to you, Molly."

"Yes," Mom agreed. "It's your decision." Even though her words were telling me that it was my choice, her eyes were begging me to do this for the zoo.

I looked around the room. This was it. My chance to tell the truth—and disappoint everybody.

"I have an idea." Helene spoke up suddenly. "We should have the monkey at the opening."

"She's an orangutan," Mom corrected Helene.

Mr. Edward's mouth dropped open. "That creature?" he asked. "Impossible. I will not have this gorilla in the same room with my priceless treasures."

"But Mr. Edward, the—"

He shook his head. "I don't want to hear it."

Helene leaned forward and whispered something in Mr. Edward's ear. I could have sworn I heard the words *television coverage* in there. As she talked, Mr. Edward alternately frowned and smiled.

Finally he nodded, then spoke to all of us.

"Mrs. Miles."

"Dr. Miles," Mom corrected him.

"Of course," Mr. Edward purred. "Dr. Miles." He took a deep breath. "If the monkey—"

"Orangutan," Mom repeated.

Mr. Edward nodded. "My point exactly. If your chimpanzee can attend the opening, it would help us all, I think. Additional press coverage never hurts."

Mom smiled. "I think it would be great, too." I could tell she was thinking about how she could sneak in a few interviews to ask people to help save the orangutans.

"And of course, we'd want your whole family to come," Helene added. "If you can."

"If we can? We'd be honored," Dad gushed. I'd never seen him so excited.

"And Tyler, too?" I asked. "He's my best friend." I was getting caught up in the excitement. For a moment, I forgot that all these people were going to hate me in a few short days.

"Of course." Mr. Edward nodded.

"If you're sure Zoey wouldn't be in the way," Mom said.

"No, not at all," Helene assured her.

"It's settled, then." Mr. Edward bowed again. "We will see you all next Monday night."

Helene reached into her briefcase and pulled out a white business card. "Here is the address."

"Good-bye," Mr. Edward said as he headed for the front door.

"Good-bye," my family repeated, almost as one.

"See you at school, Molly," Mrs. Hurwitz said. "We are all very proud of you," she added quietly.

And then they were gone. Dad shut the door and turned to me.

"Congratulations, Molly. Good work."

"Oh, Molly, I'm so proud of you." Mom rushed over to me. "I had no idea you were such an artist."

I smiled weakly. Neither did I.

Chapter 7

"Come on, Zoey," I pleaded. "Let's try it again."

I opened the gray envelope and pulled out an eight-by-ten black-and-white picture of Mr. Edward. It was a close-up shot. Mr. Edward's thin blond hair was slicked back, and he was staring off into the distance. You could tell he was trying to look like somebody really important.

I held the picture up. "Here he is, Zoey," I repeated for the millionth time. She was sitting on my bedroom floor, holding a paintbrush in her left hand. There was a little cup of water, a tray of watercolor paints, and a sketch pad opened to a big blank sheet of paper on the floor next to her. All she needed to do was paint the portrait.

"Look, it's Mr. Edward. You remember Mr. Edward, don't you?"

Zoey took one look at the picture, screeched, threw the paintbrush up in the air, and hid her eyes behind her hands.

I frowned. "Now, come on, Zoey. He may be a creep, but he's going to donate a whole lot of money to the zoo—*if* you do this painting. You'd like the zoo to get that money, wouldn't you?" I nodded encouragingly.

Zoey peered out from between her fingers and gave a much quieter screech.

"That's what I thought," I said. I picked up the paintbrush and held it out to her. "Here you go."

She took a little hop forward and grabbed the brush. I smiled. "That's it, Zoey. Paint the picture."

She dabbed the brush in the paint. Then she swiped the brush across the photo I was holding. Now Mr. Edward had an orange mustache.

"Zoey," I chided.

She screeched again, then moved the paintbrush across my face.

"Zoey!" I yelled. "Bad girl." I looked in the mirror. Now *I* had an orange mustache, and it clashed terribly with my red hair. "Cut it out!"

She dropped the brush, jumped onto my bed, and started hopping up and down and screeching. I threw my hands up in the air and tried hard not to scream.

I had been begging Zoey to paint this portrait since the previous Tuesday after school. And now it was Monday night. The night of the gallery opening. Our time was up, and all I had was a wastebasket full of soggy paper.

All week, Zoey had been acting like she'd never seen a paintbrush or paints before. She had absolutely no interest in painting at all. It made me wonder if Tyler and I were right about her doing the first painting. Maybe Brad had done it after all, or maybe one of his friends had played a trick on me, or . . .

No. If someone else had done it, they would have said something after Mr. Edward bought it.

Behind me I heard my bedroom window slide open. I turned just as Tyler stepped through.

"Hey," he remarked, staring at my face a second. "Nice look. I'm not sure about the color, though."

"Very funny," I said.

"Can I ask how it's going?"

"You can," I told him. "If you want me to scream."

"That bad, huh?"

"Worse." I flopped backward onto the floor and lay there without moving for at least thirty seconds.

"Come on, Molly," Tyler began. "It's not that bad. We'll think of something."

"Like what?" I asked, sitting up. "Why won't she do the portrait? She doesn't even want to look at the paints."

Zoey, sitting right across from me, screeched again and put the paintbrush in her mouth.

"Bad Zoey," Tyler scolded. He stepped forward and took the brush from her. "Here, girl." He wet his finger and wiped it across the picture of Mr. Edward, erasing the mustache. "You can paint this man's picture, can't you?"

Zoey screeched and held out her hand.

Tyler gave her back the paintbrush. She took it and dipped it into the little glass of water.

"That's it, Zoey," Tyler encouraged her. "Good girl."

Zoey took the picture of Mr. Edward from Tyler. She set it down on the ground next to the blank piece of paper I'd been trying to get her to draw on all afternoon, then hopped up and down excitedly.

Tyler looked up at me and smiled as Zoey dipped the paintbrush in the watercolors.

"Here we go," he said quietly. "She's going to paint."

I smiled and nodded back at him. Maybe he was right. Maybe this time Zoey would really paint Mr. Edward's portrait and save the day.

No such luck. The little orangutan hurled herself toward Tyler, bowling him over. He landed flat on his back. Before he could get up, she leaned forward and painted a big orange mustache on his face. We weren't getting anywhere with the painting, but we were setting a new fashion trend.

I burst out laughing. Tyler tried to look angry, but he gave up after a few seconds and started laughing, too.

"Hmmm," he muttered, sitting up. He took the paintbrush out of Zoey's hand before she had a chance to give him an orange beard. "We may need an alternative plan."

"I've already thought of one," I said, getting to my feet and going to my closet. I opened the door and pulled out another painting. "What do you think?"

Tyler frowned. "Who is that?"

"What do you mean?" I cried. "It's Mr. Edward. I spent almost all day yesterday locked in my room trying to copy Zoey's style."

Tyler stared closely at the picture. "It looks more like Michael Jordan to me."

"Very funny." I thought I'd done a pretty good job

imitating the primitive style that Mr. Edward seemed to love so much.

"Look," I said to Tyler. "See these lines here? I painted them exactly the same way Zoey did, with the same color paint."

As Tyler leaned closer to see what I was talking about, Zoey jumped up, grabbed the paintbrush out of his hand, and with a quick swipe, drew a big orange mustache across the painting.

"Oh, no," Tyler groaned.

I didn't even have the energy to yell at her anymore. I just let the drawing fall to the floor. I guess it didn't really matter how much it looked like him now.

"I think we need another plan," Tyler said.

"Don't look at me. I'm out of ideas, and we're out of time." I lay back down on my bed and shut my eyes.

"I'm going to get a drink of water," Tyler mumbled despairingly. "I'll be right back. Keep thinking."

I heard the door open and shut behind him. This whole week had been a nightmare. I kept thinking I should have told Mom and Dad about the painting. But the longer I waited, the harder it got. Now they were so excited about the gallery opening, what with all the papers talking about it and all the famous movie stars who would be there, that I couldn't bear to let them down. Even Brad was into it—Jean-Claude Van Damme was supposed to show up.

I heard the door open again as Tyler walked back in. I hadn't had any brilliant ideas while he was gone.

"Molly," he said quietly.

"What?" I asked, not bothering to open my eyes.

"Shhh. Molly, *look*," Tyler whispered excitedly.

"Go away," I told him. "Unless you've come up with the most brilliant, failure-proof plan to get this painting done, I'm not in the mood for talking."

"I haven't," Tyler said, still whispering, like he was trying hard not to wake somebody up. "But Zoey has."

"What?" I opened my eyes and sat up.

Zoey was sitting on the floor with the paintbrush in her hand. Wait—she wasn't just sitting. She was painting!

"Zoey!" I shouted. "You're doing it!"

She looked up at the sound of my voice and dropped everything. Then she ran into my closet, grabbed one of my shoes, and started chewing on it.

Tyler snatched the sketch pad off the floor. "It's him!" he exclaimed.

"Mr. Edward?" I asked excitedly.

He nodded. "But she's only halfway done."

He held the picture up for me to see. It *was* only half done, but now we knew why Zoey wouldn't do any work before. "She doesn't like people watching her," I said, finally understanding.

"Not when she's trying to paint, anyway," Tyler agreed.

"It was the same with the other painting," I remembered. "The one Mr. Edward bought. She only painted me after I fell asleep. I wish I had figured this out earlier."

Tyler looked at me. "This is too weird," he said. "So all we have to do to get her to finish is leave the room?"

I nodded. "I think so. I hope so." I looked down at Zoey, who was still chewing contentedly on my shoe. I took it out of her mouth gently. She stared up at me, big brown eyes shining.

"Come on, little sister," I whispered to her. "Don't let me down." I pulled out another picture of Mr. Edward from the gray envelope and set it down on the floor in front of her. I refilled the glass of water, picked up the paintbrush, and put them down next to the paints. Then I took the sketch pad from Tyler and set the half-finished painting of Mr. Edward down on the floor next to her.

"Come on." Tyler silently led me to the door. "We'll sneak out of here before she knows we're gone." Thankful this nightmare would soon be over, I took a step out into the hall—

And walked straight into my mother.

"Molly!" She looked down at me strangely. I looked up at her strangely, too. I'd never seen Mom so dressed up. She was wearing a short black dress and fancy earrings, and her hair was pulled back from her face. Looking at Mom now, it was hard to believe she spent her days in an ape house.

"Wow," I gasped. "You look beautiful."

"Thank you, honey. But why aren't you dressed? You know we have to leave in twenty minutes."

My mouth dropped open. "Twenty minutes?"

She held up her watch for me to look at. It said six-fifteen.

"Twenty minutes," she repeated. "Do you want me to fix your hair or help you get dressed?"

"No," I said quickly. We'd already picked out my outfit the night before, and my hair was a lost cause as far as I was concerned. "I'll be fine."

She looked over my shoulder and caught sight of Zoey sitting on the floor. Please, please don't let Mom see what Zoey's doing, I prayed silently.

"There you are, you little imp!" she cried, dropping to one knee. "Mommy has to get *you* dressed, now. Come here, Zoey!"

And before I could do anything, Zoey bolted from my room into my mother's arms. She scooped the little furball up and headed down the hall.

I breathed a huge sigh of relief. Then I walked back into my room and shut the door.

I looked at Zoey's half-finished painting, then at Tyler.

"I think we need another plan."

Chapter 8

Half an hour later, we were all on our way to the fanciest party of our lives.

You'd think that growing up in Los Angeles I would have seen movie stars every time we went shopping or went out to dinner. You might even think I'd been to a party with one or two of them. Well, you'd be wrong.

My family saw movie stars and their parties the same way everyone else in the world did—on TV. The most glamorous thing I'd ever gotten to do before tonight was go with Mom to one of the local news stations right after Zoey was born. She was there to talk about what it was like to have an orangutan living with us. But the show ran long, and Mom never got on the air. She was so mad she refused to go back. That was my one brush with show biz.

So tonight was kind of special for me. To tell you the truth, I think everybody was looking forward to schmoozing with the stars.

I couldn't feel too excited, though. Unless I could get Zoey to finish Mr. Edward's portrait, my big lie was going to be exposed, making this the worst night of my life.

"So, tell me again why you couldn't finish the painting, Molly," Mom said, turning around in the front seat. Dad was driving, and Tyler and I were in the seats behind them. Brad and Zoey were in the seats behind us. We were probably the only people going to this opening in a minivan instead of a stretch limousine.

"I had a hard time doing Mr. Edward's portrait from a picture, Mom," I told her. "That's why I want to finish it with him right in front of me."

"It *is* how all the famous portrait artists do it," Tyler added.

Dad nodded. "You don't think you'll be too nervous in front of all those people?"

"I will," I agreed. "That's why I need about half an hour of Mr. Edward's time alone."

"I wish you'd told us this before, Molly," Mom said in a worried voice. "I don't think it's a good idea to spring it on Mr. Edward like this. He doesn't seem the kind of person who likes surprises."

Brad leaned forward. "I'll bet he's going to be mad," he cackled.

"No sense worrying about it now," Dad said matter-of-factly. He looked at me in the rearview mirror. "I hope you know what you're doing, young lady. That's a lot of pressure to put on yourself."

"Oh, I'm not worried," I said lightly, trying to sound as confident as I could.

"Well, that makes one of us," Tyler piped up. Everybody laughed at that. It kind of eased the tension, though really, I was *very* worried.

Only Tyler and I knew that getting Mr. Edward to agree to leave the gallery opening long enough to get his portrait done was only half the battle. We had to get him to sit with his eyes closed, and somehow not let him see that it was Zoey doing the painting!

"Whoa," Dad exclaimed, slowing down. "Would you look at that."

I leaned forward in my seat to see what he was so excited about and was momentarily blinded by a dazzling array of lights. It looked like a UFO had landed in the middle of the street.

Not that the amount of lights was a big surprise. Mr. Edward's gallery was on Rodeo Drive in Beverly Hills, the richest and ritziest street in the world. And tonight it looked like Mr. Edward was hosting the most expensive party in the world. There were limousines everywhere, and it seemed as if a million flashbulbs were going off at the same time. I turned for a moment and thought I spotted Jean-Claude Van Damme dashing into the gallery entrance as we pulled up.

"Your keys, sir," a man in a red uniform droned, leaning into Dad's window. He eyed our minivan with barely concealed dismay.

"Cool," Tyler remarked as we climbed out of the car. "Valet parking. This is the big time."

"Thanks for pointing out the obvious," I told him. "Didn't the five hundred limousines ahead of us tip you off?"

There was a big banner hanging across the second

floor of the building. I leaned all the way back, straining to read what it said.

EDWARD GALLERIES
GRAND OPENING EXHIBITION: THE PRIMITIVES
FOR THE BENEFIT OF THE LOS ANGELES ZOO

Zoey, who was in the carrier on Brad's shoulders, squawked as we made our way past the huge crowd outside the gallery. It was like the Academy Awards or something. There were red velvet ropes along the entrance to the gallery to keep the regular people away from all the celebrities. Right now, I was one of the famous people.

"So this is what it's like to be a movie star." Brad smiled and waved to the crowd. "It feels kind of weird to have all these people gawking at us."

"You're telling me," I said as I stopped to pose for a picture.

At the entrance to the gallery, a big man was checking names on the guest list. Dad walked up to him and said in his most official voice, "Dr. Charles Miles and family."

The man looked down the first page of his list, then the second, then the third. Finally, on the last page, he found our names and crossed them off. He looked at Dad for a moment, then mumbled, "Step inside, please."

Inside the gallery, it was even more of a madhouse. The foyer was brimming with famous people in expensive clothes. They were sipping champagne and chatting in small groups. One group of people was having a conversation about a blob of shiny metal that was perched on top of a marble pedestal. They were all gesturing with their hands and saying things like "What a beautiful line," and "You can almost feel the artist's grief." I took another quick look at the sculpture. I was right the first time. It was just a blob.

As we walked through the gallery, I started to get a little worried. How was I even going to find Mr. Edward in this place, much less get him to sit still for a few minutes so we could do the painting?

"Molly!" I turned and saw Helene walking toward us. She was dressed in a black silk cocktail dress. Her big diamond necklace glittered in the light. Even though she looked great, she still smelled like she had bathed in that deadly perfume.

"We're very glad to see you—and everyone else, of course," she added, nodding at my family and Tyler. Then she looked around. "Where is your painting?"

"It's in here." I smiled, holding up the big bag that held my sketchbook and all my supplies. "But I haven't finished it."

Helene's face fell. "What?"

"I haven't finished it *yet,* I should have said. I couldn't do it from Mr. Edward's picture," I explained quickly. "I need him to sit for me."

"Here? *Now?*" She shook her head. "Impossible."

"It won't take more than ten minutes. I promise."

Helene looked at me suspiciously. "Wait here," she said finally. "I will bring Mr. Edward."

I nodded and watched as she disappeared into the churning crowd.

"Molly?" Mom asked. "Is everything all right?"

"Great," I said, putting on my best smile.

"We're sunk," Tyler whispered in my ear.

"Relax," I whispered back. "Enjoy yourself."

There were dozens of paintings hanging on the walls, and sculptures were scattered everywhere throughout the room. Everyone in the gallery looked like a movie star, and there were waiters in tuxedos moving through the crowd with huge trays of food and drinks. Mom even gave me a sip of her champagne, which made a kind of delicate little fizz on my tongue. I liked it. I would have been happy to just stand there all night and take in the sights.

"Well, I don't know about the rest of you," Mom said finally. "But I think I'm going to mingle a little. I thought I saw Jean-Claude Van Damme in that corner over there."

"Right," Dad chirped. "I'll keep an eye out for Cindy Crawford."

"Very funny," she murmured, turning to go.

"Hey, Mom, could I come with you?" Brad asked. Zoey was perched on Brad's shoulders. A waiter walked by them with a tray of mouthwatering hors d'oeuvres balanced on his outstretched hand. As the waiter turned to one of the guests, Zoey kissed his head, then snatched a handful of treats off the tray. The waiter looked around, trying to figure out why his head was covered in spit.

"I could take Zoey," Tyler volunteered as he held his arms out.

Mom thought for a moment before she agreed. "Okay, Tyler. But be careful to keep her away from all the photographers. I don't want her to get too excited yet."

I smiled. Zoey was scheduled to stand in front of all the photographers when Mr. Edward unveiled the portrait, but Mom would be with her then to keep her in line. As for right now, things couldn't have worked out any better if we'd planned them.

"Tyler will take good care of her," I told Mom. "I'll make sure of it."

"Yeah, I'll wait here with Molly for Mr. Edward," Tyler said. "You go on and have a good time. I'll keep Zoey quiet."

We watched as they wandered off. A minute later, Mr. Edward dove through the crowd and sauntered over to us. Helene was right behind him.

"Ah, there you are, Molly," he cooed. He was dressed in a black turtleneck, black pants, black sport jacket, and (of course) his black beret. "Helene tells me there is a problem with the painting."

"No problem," I assured him. "I just need a few minutes of your time, sir, so I can finish it."

"You don't have it now?" Mr. Edward asked flatly. I could almost see steam coming out of his ears. "I have promised the press people here a surprise."

"I wanted to do a good job for you, sir," I explained as politely as I could. "And it's not the same painting from a picture. As a fellow artist, I'm sure you understand."

He glared at me, then his expression softened.

"Of course," he said quietly. "I do understand. You want the real me, what is in here"—he tapped his chest—"not what the photographer has shown. I should have known that you could not capture the real me from a photograph."

He thought a moment. "There is a workshop upstairs. We can create there without people disturbing us. Come."

Without waiting for a reply, he spun on his heel and started to walk off.

"Come on, Tyler," I said, picking up my bag. "Let's go."

Mr. Edward turned around quickly and shook his head.

"Oh, no. Not the monkey. You can't bring the monkey."

"What?" My jaw dropped to the floor.

"I can't have people—or animals—watching me while I work," he argued.

"But *I'm* the one working," I reasoned. "Having Zoey there won't bother me. In fact, she sometimes inspires me." I silently wondered how many lies I could tell before my head would explode.

"Young lady," he said sternly. "For you to capture the essence of Georges Edward in a painting, I must bare my soul. To do that, I must concentrate and bring forth the part of me that is the most . . ." He paused, searching for just the right word. "Me. How can I do that with an audience that is not in sync with my inner rhythm? It is, of course, impossible." He smiled his fake-teeth smile at me. "So, you see?"

"Uhhh . . ." I frowned. "Not exactly, sir."

"No monkey," he said curtly, and walked away.

Helene put a hand on Tyler's arm. "No monkey," she repeated.

I shared a worried glance with Tyler as I slowly followed Mr. Edward.

Now what?

Chapter 9

Mr. Edward led me upstairs to the back of the gallery. The sign on the door at the top of the stairs said WORKSHOP. PLEASE DO NOT DISTURB THE ARTIST WHILE HE IS CREATING. Mr. Edward unlocked the door and led me into a small room. It was pretty bare, except for a big round table, half a dozen chairs, and a tall artist's easel that stood in a corner by a large window. One wall was lined with shelves filled with painting supplies. Lots of small paintings and sketches were tacked to another wall.

"I will sit here," he decided, taking one of the chairs and dragging it to the far corner of the room. "You sit over there." Mr. Edward pointed to the round table. I took another chair, pulled it up to the table, and sat down heavily.

"Well," he said, rubbing his hands together. "We have ten minutes. Let us make art!"

"Yes, sir," I replied nervously. I pulled my supplies out of the bag, arranged them on the table, then walked over to the sink to get a glass of water. I came back to the chair, set down the water, and tentatively picked up the paintbrush.

Mr. Edward puffed out his chest and sat up tall.

"You may begin when you are ready, Molly," he commanded. "Remember, heroic."

"Yes, sir," I said.

"But not too heroic," he added.

I took a deep breath and dipped the paintbrush into the water.

Here goes nothing, I thought. I held the brush poised over the paper.

"Noble more than heroic," Mr. Edward decided, looking at me out of the corner of his eye.

I nodded just as there was a knock on the door. Helene walked in with Tyler and Zoey.

"What are you doing here?" Mr. Edward asked impatiently as he eyed Zoey. "Can't you see we are in the process of creating?"

"The monkey, Mr. Edward," Helene explained. "It was getting very upset."

"Orangutan," I told her. "Zoey is an orangutan." I don't know why I was bothering to try and correct them anymore—she and Mr. Edward didn't seem to hear me, anyway.

"The boy told me seeing Molly would calm it down," Helene continued.

"It seems to have worked," Tyler remarked. "She's much better already."

"She was trying to eat the Kennedy sculptures," Helene added in a horrified tone.

"The sculptures?" Mr. Edward froze. "They're all right, aren't they?"

"We stopped her just in time," Helene assured him. Mr. Edward sank back in his chair, relieved.

I smiled gratefully at Tyler. Later, I'd have to ask him what he'd done to get Zoey riled up. But for right now all I had to do was get my little monkey—er, orangutan—to finish this portrait.

"I'm ready," I said.

"I don't know if I can do it with that ape in the room," Mr. Edward mumbled impatiently to himself. "I just don't know."

I sighed and looked at Tyler. I knew he was thinking the same thing I was. We had two very temperamental artists to deal with. If this painting ever got finished, it would be a miracle.

"Well, you could close your eyes and pretend she's not here," I suggested.

"You can do the painting with my eyes closed?" He looked like he didn't believe me.

"Yes," I said. "In fact, I'd prefer to. I think I'll get less nervous that way. It's kind of hard for me to be painting the portrait of such a famous artist." I swore right then and there that if I ever made it out of this mess, I'd never lie again.

"Oh. Very well, then," Mr. Edward said, obviously pleased by all my flattering remarks. "Helene, you'd better get back downstairs. Try to keep everyone from leaving. Ask the pianist to play something lively." He sat back down on his chair, struck the same pose he had before, and then closed his eyes.

I smiled. This was going to be easy.

I waved Tyler over, and he handed me Zoey. I set her down on the chair and handed her my paintbrush.

"Not too heroic," Mr. Edward repeated, straightening his beret.

"Of course not," I said.

"Let's go hide behind there," I whispered to Tyler, pointing to a stack of canvases in the far corner of the room. We made our way over there on tiptoe and crouched behind them. After a minute, I peeked around the side.

Zoey was painting!

"She's doing it," I whispered to Tyler, ducking back down. "She's really doing it!"

"All right!" he mouthed, peering out around the other edge of the canvases. "I knew she . . ." His voice trailed off. "Uh-oh."

"Uh-oh?" I shook my head. What uh-oh?

Then I looked out again and saw what uh-oh Tyler was talking about. Zoey had jumped out of the chair. Now she was toddling toward Mr. Edward, paintbrush in hand.

I stood up and tried to wave her back over to the table before she painted a big orange mustache on his face.

Zoey looked at me and screeched loudly.

"What!" Mr. Edward opened his eyes and sat bolt upright in his chair. He looked around the room, first at Zoey, then at me. "What is going on here? What is that monkey doing?"

I opened my mouth to speak but couldn't think of anything to say.

"It has stolen your paintbrush!" Mr. Edward guessed, standing. He advanced on Zoey. "Give me that paintbrush, you ape. You are interfering with art!" He lunged at her.

Zoey screeched, stuck her tongue out at him, and jumped backward. Tyler and I darted out from behind the easel at the same instant and grabbed for her. We ran smack into each other and crashed our heads together.

"Ow!" I shrieked as I staggered and fell. Tyler crumpled into a groaning heap on the floor.

I rubbed my throbbing head as I looked up. Zoey jumped up onto the easel, and then onto Mr. Edward's back.

"Ahh!" he shouted. "Get it off! Get it off!"

He stumbled backward into his chair as he tried to pry her toes off his shoulders.

Zoey grabbed the beret off Mr. Edward's head and bounded to the opposite corner of the room. She sat on the window ledge beside a shelf full of painting supplies. I made a mental note to buy Zoey her own beret when this nightmare was over.

I struggled to my feet just as Mr. Edward got out of his chair and moved toward Zoey again. He was seething with rage, and he looked like he was ready to strangle all of us.

"That's a silk beret, you mutant monkey," he screamed. "You give that back to me or . . ."

Mr. Edward never got a chance to finish his sentence. What happened next seemed to take forever, even though it was all over in a few seconds. Zoey grabbed a can of paint off the shelf next to her, wound up like a baseball pitcher, and threw it. Brad would have been very proud of her delivery.

The can hit Mr. Edward right on top of the head. His eyes opened wide for a brief instant. Then he fell over like he'd been shot.

Chapter 10

Tyler and I stood frozen, too stunned to move. Mr. Edward was sprawled on the floor in front of us. He wasn't moving.

Zoey looked down at Mr. Edward and blew him a raspberry. Then she jumped off the window ledge, pounced on his chest, and began bouncing up and down.

"Oh, this is great," Tyler groaned in disbelief. "We've killed him."

"Zoey, stop that!" I yelled. I pulled her off Mr. Edward, who still wasn't moving. "Is—is he dead?" I stammered.

Tyler knelt down next to Mr. Edward and put his head to his chest.

"I hear his heartbeat," Tyler said.

I let out a sigh of relief. For a moment I had visions of Zoey and me sharing a prison cell until I was old and wrinkled.

"Well, let's wake him up," I told Tyler. "Splash cold water on him or something."

Tyler frowned. "I don't think you're supposed to do that with people who have head injuries."

I shook my head. "That's wrong. People with head

injuries have to stay awake. They're not supposed to go to sleep."

"Really?" Tyler frowned. "I thought it was the other way around."

He and I looked at each other.

"I guess I don't really know for sure," I moaned. "But Brad would know."

"Do you think he'll help you?" Tyler asked.

"Of course he will," I replied. "I'm his little sister."

"Exactly," Tyler said. "He might do it if we take over his chores for the next month."

"He'll help me," I assured Tyler. "You just keep an eye on Zoey."

"All right," he said. "But hurry back. If Mr. Edward wakes up, I don't want to be the only human here."

I bolted out of the workroom and ran downstairs as quickly as I could. The gallery was even more crowded than before, if that was possible.

"Molly!"

I turned around and saw Helene walking toward me.

I smiled at her, then turned and walked as fast as I could in the other direction. I didn't have time to answer any questions. I didn't really have time even to be here, honestly. I should call an ambulance. I should tell Dad, not Brad. I should—

I walked right into a waiter carrying a tray full of drinks, knocking it out of his hand and onto the floor. The tray and all the crystal champagne glasses made a huge crashing noise as they landed on the polished marble floor.

After the din of breaking glass subsided, I noticed how quiet the room had become. I looked up and saw everyone in the gallery looking at me.

"My fault," I announced. "Mine, not his." I pointed at the waiter, then bent down to try and help him pick up the mess.

"That's not necessary, miss," he said, smiling at me. It was the kind of polite smile you give somebody when what you really want to do is kill her.

"I'm sorry," I whispered. "Really I am."

"Nice move, Red."

I turned and saw Brad standing behind me, grinning. He knew how much I hated that nickname, and normally I would've let him have it for calling me that. But not now. I needed his help.

"Brad! I've been looking all over for you," I began. "I need you to come with me. Now. Please." I grabbed his arm and began to pull.

He smiled. "You found Keanu Reeves!"

"No, no." I shook my head. "This is more important than any movie star. I need your help." I stood up on my toes and whispered in his ear. "It's a matter of life or death."

He looked at me funny. "Sure it is."

I raised my hand. "Cross my heart and hope to die, I swear it."

"Wow." Brad studied me a minute. "You are serious." I nodded.

"Does this have something to do with the painting?" he asked.

"In a way," I mumbled. "I mean, yes."

Then I explained the whole thing to him—well, the part about Zoey beaning Mr. Edward, anyway.

"You sure know how to get in trouble, Molly," he remarked as we were making our way upstairs. I got the feeling he admired that about me in a strange kind of way. "So what was Zoey doing with the paintbrush?"

"Er . . ." I didn't know what to say to that. Luckily I didn't have to stall for too long, because just then we reached the workshop. I opened the door, and we ducked inside.

The scene was pretty much the way I'd left it, except that Zoey was chewing on Mr. Edward's silk beret. Tyler was kneeling over him, his ear bent to Mr. Edward's chest.

"His heart's still beating," Tyler announced. "And his blood pressure's eighty."

"Eighty?" Brad asked. "What do you mean, eighty?"

I walked over to Zoey and took the beret from her. She grabbed it right back and threw it on the floor. Then she stuck her tongue out and turned her back toward me.

"Bad girl," I scolded. Zoey ignored me.

"Eighty beats per minute," Tyler stated. "I think that's normal."

"That's not how you do blood pressure." Brad rolled his eyes. "It's a good thing you came to get me, Molly."

He knelt down next to Tyler and looked at Mr. Edward. "He's out cold, all right. What did Zoey hit him with?"

"This," Tyler said. He held up the little can of paint, which had a dent in one side now, then tossed it to Brad.

"Wow," Brad exclaimed, hefting the can in one hand. "Zoey must have great aim. I think he's going to be okay, though."

"He'll live?" I asked.

"Oh, yeah. He'll live." A small smile formed on Brad's lips. "If I were you guys, though, I wouldn't want to be around when he wakes up."

Just then, right on cue, Mr. Edward started groaning and mumbling to himself.

"What's he saying?" I asked Brad.

"I don't know." He leaned in closer to listen. "Something about income tax, I think."

Brad stood up and dusted off his pants. "I think he'll be fine. But he's going to have a nasty bump on his head."

Tyler snapped his fingers. "I know what we can do about that." He ran over and picked the beret up off the floor from where Zoey had thrown it. He fluffed it up, wiped off the orangutan drool, and laid it carefully on Mr. Edward's head.

"Good as new," Tyler said.

Brad nodded and started walking toward the door. "Well, good luck. I'm going to go find some more movie stars." He stopped at the table and picked something up off it.

"Is this your painting, Molly?" he asked, holding up my sketchbook. "It's nice."

"I don't believe it!" I exclaimed.

"What?" Tyler asked, turning.

We both stood there for a minute, staring at the painting. It was finished.

After all that, Zoey had actually finished the portrait! I was so excited, I lost control of myself.

"It's done!" I screamed. I bent down and kissed her. "You did it! You did it!"

"Uh, Molly," Tyler muttered. He was facing the front of the room, and he had a funny expression on his face. "Calm down."

"But Zoey did it, Tyler," I cried. "She finished the painting!"

"*Zoey* finished the painting?"

I froze in my tracks. That wasn't Tyler's voice.

I turned around. My parents were standing in the doorway, staring at us openmouthed. Mom was the first to speak.

"I couldn't have heard you correctly, Molly. Would you repeat that?"

"Uhhh . . ." I was racking my brain, trying to come up with some kind of explanation.

Dad shut the door to the workroom and stood in front of it, hands folded across his chest.

"Maybe you'd better tell us what exactly is going on here." He spoke very slowly, and that meant I was in big trouble.

Chapter 11

I was saved from answering my father by Mr. Edward. He started groaning again, much louder this time.

"Ohhh," he moaned, getting up on his elbows. "I feel as if the Eiffel Tower has fallen on my head."

My dad looked behind me, saw Mr. Edward, and hurried over to him.

"Are you hurt?" he asked, his voice filled with concern. He knelt down next to Mr. Edward and helped him into a sitting position.

"He's all right, Dad," Brad said. "I don't think he has a concussion."

My father looked up at him. "And when did you get your medical degree?"

Brad turned bright red.

"Are *you* a doctor?" Mr. Edward asked, rubbing his head and staring at my father.

"Don't you recognize me?" Dad spoke quietly. "I'm Charles Miles, Molly's father."

Mr. Edward rubbed his eyes as he tried to focus on Dad's face. "I think so," he mumbled. "Charles Miles. Yes, it's all coming back to me now." He looked around the room at Brad, then me, and finally at Zoey.

"Aha! There she is!" he shouted. "Oh, my head!"

At the sound of Mr. Edward's angry voice, Zoey screeched and hopped into my mother's arms.

"That monkey—"

"Orangutan," Mom corrected.

"Monkey," Mr. Edward screamed, using his whole arm to point at Zoey. "That monkey tried to kill me!"

"What?" Mom cried. "Zoey wouldn't hurt a fly. You must be mistaken."

Mr. Edward shook his head before he remembered that it hurt. He grimaced, then held his throbbing skull in his hands. "It was deliberate on the monkey's part, I am quite sure, madam. It threw the paint can—"

"She," Mom corrected him. "She threw the paint can."

"Yes," Mr. Edward agreed. "You are correct. The ape threw it—right at me!"

"Nonsense." Mom sniffed.

"Now, Sara," Dad said calmly. "Let the man finish his story."

"It was an accident," Tyler stated. "Zoey just—"

"Charles, it's ridiculous," Mom interrupted. "You know Zoey simply wouldn't do such a thing."

"Oh, no?" Mr. Edward glared up at her. He pulled the beret off his head and exposed the large purple bruise on his forehead. Because he had really straight, thin blond hair, it was very visible. "I suppose this is ridiculous, too!"

"Oh, dear," Mom whispered.

"Ouch." Dad winced. He leaned in closer to examine Mr. Edward's head. "That's got to hurt. Let me take a look at it."

Mr. Edward brushed my father aside as he struggled to his feet. "I will get my personal physician, sir, thank you very much just the same." He put the beret back on his head, grimacing as he pulled the soft silk over his bruised forehead.

"Molly, what happened here?" Mom demanded. "What did Zoey really do?"

"Well, she did throw the paint can," I admitted. "But it wasn't really her fault, Mom. I can explain everything. You see—"

"You explain all you want, young lady. I'm calling the police," Mr. Edward raged. "That monkey belongs in a cage!"

"You can't call the police!" I cried.

"Can't I?" Mr. Edward asked. "This is the second time I have been assaulted by this ape."

"It was hardly assault," Dad reasoned. He was trying to play the diplomat, a role he was usually very good at. "Now, Mr. Edward, let's just take a deep breath and try to relax for a minute."

Mr. Edward, though, wasn't going to be calmed down right then. Not by my dad, not by anybody.

"I will give you your minute," he seethed, folding his arms across his chest, "if you will give me one good reason why I should not call the police and have this monkey—"

"Orangutan!" Mom and I yelled at the same time.

"Ape," Mr. Edward continued. "Why I should not have it put in a cage where it belongs!"

"Because you just paid her a thousand dollars to do your portrait!" I blurted out.

The whole room, which had been full of screaming, angry people a minute ago, was suddenly quiet. All eyes turned to me.

"What did you say?" Mr. Edward asked haughtily.

"Now we're in for it," Tyler mumbled.

Dad turned and gave me his best "Molly Miles what have you been up to?" look.

"Is th-that what you were saying before, when we came in?" Mom stammered. "Did Zoey really do the painting?"

I nodded slowly.

"I think I need to sit down," Mom said shakily.

Just then, the door to the workroom opened, and Helene stepped in.

"Mr. Edward, is everything all right?" she asked. "People downstairs are wondering—"

"No, Helene, everything is not all right," Mr. Edward interrupted. He pulled over one of the chairs and sat down, too. "Everything is very far from being all right."

"Okay, Molly," Dad said evenly. "Why don't you start at the beginning, and tell us everything that happened."

"Yes, sir." I took a deep breath, then began to tell my story. I started with Dad's mix-up when he framed Zoey's painting, and continued right through to the portrait session tonight.

I had spilled my guts in less than five minutes.

There was a moment of silence, then the room erupted with noise again. Everybody was trying to speak at once.

"I want my money back," Mr. Edward was yelling. "Give me my money back. I will have none of this trickery."

Dad was still trying to calm Mr. Edward down by playing the peacemaker. Mom was bouncing Zoey on her knee and telling her she was the best little orangutan artist in the whole world. Tyler was filling Brad in on more of the details.

I didn't have anything to say, but I was getting very worried. Helene and Mr. Edward were talking now, and he was getting angrier and angrier.

"Mr. Edward," I begged. "Please, please don't send Zoey to jail! It's not her fault! I should have said something earlier. Take me instead."

He looked up at me and glared. I had never seen anyone that angry. For a minute I had a sick feeling that he really would call the police and have me arrested.

"No one's going to jail," Dad said reasonably. "Zoey's going to be fine. But we do have some things to work out here, Molly. I think you kids should go downstairs so the grown-ups can figure out the best way to handle this."

"No one is going anywhere!"

Helene's voice boomed across the small studio. I would never have thought she could yell so loudly. As I turned to face her, I wondered if my parents would ground me until I graduated from college.

And then Helene did the last thing I would have expected.

She smiled at me.

"Zoey *is* going to be fine, Molly," she said, her voice filled with excitement. "In fact, we've decided—"

"If you don't mind," Mr. Edward interrupted, standing up. "I will announce this decision." He cleared his throat and began to speak.

"In light of the unique capabilities of this, uh"—he looked at Zoey—"orangutan, I do not feel it necessary to bother the police with this matter at this time. Furthermore, because I am a *very* generous person, and because I do not wish to have any bad publicity about the gallery opening, I have also decided to honor the terms of our original, legally binding agreement. I will donate one thousand dollars to the zoo for this portrait."

Before I could even try to figure out what he'd said, Mr. Edward grabbed the portrait off the table and walked to the door.

"Helene!" Mr. Edward called, holding the door open. "People are waiting."

"I thought you might decide something like that," Mom told Helene.

I was confused, though. "Why?"

"Paintings by an orangutan?" Helene exclaimed. "I think they might be quite unique and valuable items, Molly." She smiled at me again. "We'll be downstairs, gathering the press together to prepare them for this story. It should be quite interesting. Please come down when you're ready."

And then they were gone.

"Hey, she turned out to be a nice person," I marveled. Except for the perfume, I thought to myself.

"Most people are nice, when you get right down to it," Dad said.

"What about Mr. Edward?" I asked.

"Most," Dad repeated. "I did say most."

Mom turned to Zoey and gave her a quick cuddle. "I have the feeling you're going to be very, very famous pretty soon," she cooed.

"Primitive Art has taken on a whole new meaning." Dad laughed, shaking his head. He turned to me, and I knew he was about to give me a big lecture about what I'd done.

Then Mom leaned in close and whispered something in his ear. He nodded when she was finished.

"All right," he agreed, and gave her a kiss. He ruffled the hair on top of my head. "I'll see you both downstairs. Come on, you guys." He led Tyler and Brad to the door. They walked into the hall, and the door closed softly behind them.

It was just Mom, Zoey, and me alone in the workroom.

"Molly," Mom began.

"I know, Mom," I interrupted. "I'm really sorry. I should have—"

"No, let me finish," Mom said. "All I want to say to

you is that I hope this helps you learn a lesson. It's a lifelong lesson, and maybe you're not done learning it yet, but it's really a very simple one."

She put both hands on my shoulders, and knelt down so that we were face-to-face with each other.

"Honesty is always—*always*—the best policy." She stared into my eyes for a few seconds as if she were trying to make sure I understood what she was saying. "All right?"

"All right," I whispered, feeling a little tear come to my eye. "But I did try to tell the truth, Mom. A couple of times. It's just that no one would let me explain what happened."

I hiccuped back a sob. "Then I got worried that Mr. Edward might take his money back, and there would be no more Art Walks. Then he asked me to paint his portrait, and you and Dad were so proud of me, I just couldn't say no. And everyone got so excited when Mr. Edward invited us to the gallery opening that I didn't want to spoil everyone's fun." I stopped and took a long, shaky breath. It felt good to finally be able to say all these things to someone who was listening.

Mom put her arms around me and gently led me over to one side of the room.

"I'm sorry none of us listened to you," Mom said as she patted my back. "But everything turned out okay, you know. In fact, it was kind of funny."

I started to smile. Thinking about Mr. Edward in such a state of panic was worth everything I'd had to put up with!

"'Get that monkey out of here!'" I did my best imitation of Mr. Edward's voice. Then I laughed and pointed to the corner where Zoey had been sitting. But she was gone!

Panic gripped my stomach. After all this, where could Zoey possibly be?

"Molly." Mom put her hand on my shoulder and turned me to the other side of the room. Zoey was standing beside the table where I had laid out my painting supplies, and a paintbrush was dangling from her mouth.

"Shhhhhh!" Mom said in the loudest whisper you can imagine. "Just let her do her thing."

"Harrumph!" I snorted. "Like I haven't been trying to do just that for the last week," I mouthed silently, my words muffled by my mother's hand.

It didn't take long. A few swipes of red paint here, a few there, and some other colors mixed in just for fun. And then, after spilling what was left of the yellow paint on herself, the great orange artist was done.

She looked up at us, held out her arms, and squeaked until Mom walked over to pick her up. Personally, I didn't want to get near Zoey while the paint was still dripping from her fur, so I gave them lots of room and went to look at the picture.

It was amazing. I didn't know if what I thought I was seeing was what Zoey had meant to paint, but there were two different-sized vertical green lines with red at the top, and one smaller all-red, oval-shaped thing between them. And I swear it looked like the red thing was holding on to the big and small green things. To me it looked liked a picture of Zoey standing between Mom and me. (I don't know why she made us green, but we both do have a pile of red hair on top!)

"Mom, look at this." I held the painting up to show her. "Do you think . . ." I didn't even want to finish the sentence. It was too crazy. Could Zoey have painted a picture of us?

"I don't know, honey," Mom answered absent-mindedly while she used an unstretched canvas to wipe some of the paint off Zoey. "But no matter what it is, I think it's beautiful."

Mom used to say that about some of my scribbled artwork when I was little, too. I guess love really is blind.

"Maybe Mr. Edward will offer us more money for it," I thought out loud.

Zoey screeched and grabbed for me. Or was it the painting I held in my hand?

"Okay, Zoey," I assured her. "No matter how much he offers, we'll keep this one just for us." I shook my head. "I was only kidding, anyway."

Zoey's screeching settled down into a contented chirp. She buried her face in the warm place between Mom's neck and shoulder.

"Come on, then," Mom said as she walked toward the door. "Let's get out of here while the two of us are still relatively paint-free. I want to introduce you and your fuzzy orange sister to Jean-Claude Van Damme. Maybe there's a part in his next movie for a red-haired girl and her adorable orangutan."

I smiled as I closed the door behind me. If Mom thought I was going to spend twelve hours a day on a movie set with Zoey, she was nuts. Then again, I guess our family wasn't really all that normal.

As we walked down the stairs, Zoey looked over Mom's shoulder and smiled at me. Maybe she wasn't perfect, but I was glad Zoey was my baby sister.

Zoey & Me

Don't miss any of
Zoey's zany adventures!

_____ 0-8167-4211-1
There's an Orangutan in My Bathtub $2.95

_____ 0-8167-4278-2
Who Gave My Orangutan a Paintbrush? $3.50

_____ 0-8167-4426-2
Keep Your Hands Off My Orangutan! $2.95

*Available at your favorite bookstore . . .
or use this form to order by mail.*

Please send me the books I have checked above. I am enclosing $_____
(please add $2.00 for shipping and handling). Send check or money order payable
to Troll Communications — no cash or C.O.D.s, please — to Troll
Communications, Customer Service, 2 Lethbridge Plaza, Mahwah, NJ 07430.

Name_____

Address _____

City _____State_____ZIP _____

Age _____ Where did you buy this book? _____

Please allow approximately four weeks for delivery. Offer good in the U.S. only. Sorry, mail
orders are not available to residents of Canada. Price subject to change.